SALMA

Writes a Book

Story by
Danny Ramadan

Art by
Anna Bron

annick press
toronto · berkeley

Cover art by Anna Bron, designed by Sam Tse
Interior design by Sam Tse
Cover and interior based on the series design by Paul Covello

Edited by Claire Caldwell
Copy edited by Kateri Couture-Latour
Proofread by Eleanor Gasparik

Annick Press Ltd.

We acknowledge the support of the Canada Council for the Arts and
the Ontario Arts Council, and the participation of the Government of Canada/
la participation du gouvernement du Canada for our publishing activities.

ONTARIO ARTS COUNCIL
CONSEIL DES ARTS DE L'ONTARIO
an Ontario government agency
un organisme du gouvernement de l'Ontario

Library and Archives Canada Cataloguing in Publication

Title: Salma writes a book / story by Danny Ramadan ; art by Anna Bron.
Names: Ramadan, Ahmad Danny, author. | Bron, Anna, 1989- illustrator.
Identifiers: Canadiana (print) 20230154867 | Canadiana (ebook) 20230154875 |
ISBN 9781773218021 (hardcover) | ISBN 9781773218038 (softcover) | ISBN
9781773218045 (HTML) | ISBN 9781773218052 (PDF)
Classification: LCC PS8635.A4613 S27 2023 | DDC jC813/.6—dc23

Published in the U.S.A. by Annick Press (U.S.) Ltd.
Distributed in Canada by University of Toronto Press.
Distributed in the U.S.A. by Publishers Group West.

Printed in Canada

annickpress.com
dannyramadan.com
annabron.com

Also available as an e-book. Please visit annickpress.com/ebooks for more details.

To my husband, Matthew.
With you, I am always proud.
–D.R.

To Dana and Tommy.
–A.B.

Table of Contents

Chapter 1

Salma fills in the last bits of sky in her family portrait. The blue goes nicely with Vancouver's green forests stretching in the background; the Fraser River twirls throughout. The mountains, tall and capped with white snow, tower over the scene. She adds a beautiful mosaic border around her drawing, then decorates it with jasmine flowers and little birds. In the center, Salma draws her mama and baba holding hands.

Salma adds herself beside Baba, with a big smile on her face.

Beside Mama, Salma draws her uncle, Khalou Dawood.

"Salma, can you go downstairs and help your baba?" Mama says from the kitchen. Salma leaves the coloring pencils scattered around her, takes a final look at her work, and rushes out of her room.

"I am really excited for my khalou's visit," she says as she pulls on her rain boots.

"Me, too!" Mama holds Salma's jacket open so Salma can get her arms into the sleeves. "I haven't seen my brother in so long!"

Salma slips into the hallway and runs to the elevator.

Salma has heard about her uncle, Khalou Dawood,

for as long as she can remember. He left Syria and came to Canada years before she was born. He studied at a university in a faraway city called Toronto, then found a job and stayed. But Khalou Dawood moved to Vancouver recently, and now he's finally visiting them in their new home.

The elevator opens on the garage level. Salma spots Baba pulling the last bag out of the trunk of their car. He hands it to Salma, and she is surprised it's not full of groceries like all the others. The cloth bag has Salma's favorite bookstore logo on it.

"Wow!" Salma says. "Did you buy me new coloring books?"

"No, Salma, these books are for your mother and me."

Salma sneaks a look at the titles. She can read them but isn't sure what they mean.

"Have you ever met my khalou, Baba?" Salma asks as they ride the elevator back to their floor.

"I did, once, a long time ago—way before you were born," Baba says.

Salma has never had an uncle before. At least not nearby. Her friends tell her of the adventures their favorite uncles take them on, like a day trip to the amusement park, or a night drive to a kids' theater show, and the many candies and toys they offer. Riya's uncle even lets her play her favorite songs loud in his car when he drives them somewhere. Now, Salma will get to do all of this, too. And it will be even more fun, because Khalou Dawood will be the best khalou in the whole wide world.

"Why hasn't he visited us before?" Salma asks. Toronto might be far, but it's not as far as Syria.

Ayman's uncle even visited once from Prince Edward Island, and that's so far away, the sun rises there four hours before it does in Vancouver.

"You will have to ask your mama." The elevator doors open, and she follows her baba out.

Salma takes the books to her parents' bedroom. Then, she sets the table while Mama organizes ingredients next to a big cooking pot, preparing for the big meal.

"Why hasn't my khalou visited us before, Mama?" Salma asks, but Mama doesn't answer right away. Salma looks over and sees Mama standing still, holding the lid of the pot. Her eyes look faraway and her lips quiver.

"Mama?" Salma says.

Mama snaps out of her trance. She takes a deep

breath, puts the lid down, then sprinkles some spices on the meal. But she still doesn't answer Salma. She is about to ask her question again when Mama finally looks her in the eyes.

"When we were young," Mama says, "your khalou and I used to play pranks on your grandparents all the time."

"Oh, so that's where Salma gets her pranks from!" Baba jokes from the couch.

"No. My pranks are all original," Salma teases. "No one is a better prankster than me!"

Everyone laughs. Salma smiles, too, proud of her joke. But Mama still has not answered her question. There is something her parents don't want to talk about. She knows it's not polite to insist, but curiosity is overwhelming her.

A few hours later, the smell of fried eggplants and minced meat fills the apartment.

"I'll get it!" Salma shouts when the doorbell rings. She swings open the door and finds her khalou on the other side. She recognizes him from photos: he is tall, with brown skin glimmering like sand on the riverbank, and wide black eyes. She jumps into his arms, and he gives her a big squeeze.

"Salma! What a big girl you are!"

"I am the tallest girl in my class!" she announces proudly.

"I am sure you are also the smartest." He pats her hair.

"Dawood!" Mama passes Salma and hugs her brother. She kisses him on both cheeks, then pulls him in for a second hug.

"It has been too long." Khalou shakes Baba's hand. The family gathers in the living room, and Salma sits right by her khalou's side. She listens as the family chitchats, laughs at her baba's jokes, and watches her mama dote on her brother.

"I wish I'd met you years ago, Khalou," Salma says, and Khalou pulls her in for a hug. Finally, Salma asks the question that's been on her mind. "Why haven't you come to visit before?"

The grown-ups go silent. Baba's face is concerned, and Mama's has the same look she had earlier: like she's remembering something sad. Khalou hesitates, then finally says, "You see, Salma, your mama and I had a big fight."

"We don't talk about this anymore," Mama interrupts. Her voice is a bit too loud.

"Salma is growing up in Canada, sister," Khalou insists. "I won't be the last man she meets who is married to another m——"

"No. Please stop talking." Mama interrupts again. This time, there is anger in her eyes, as if Khalou broke her favorite vase or spilled rice all over the

living room floor.

Khalou takes a deep breath. He looks at Mama as if he is about to say something, then rests his eyes on Salma and gives her a small smile. "Yes, you are right," he says to Mama. "We won't talk about this."

"Let's eat, then," Mama says quickly.

At the dinner table, it's as if someone broke glass dishes all over the floor, and everyone is afraid to step on a sharp piece. Salma wiggles in her seat. She imagined her first meeting with Khalou to be filled with happy moments, but instead it's tense. What are the grown-ups not telling her?

Chapter 2

After Khalou's first visit, Salma tried asking Mama why she seemed angry at Khalou, but she always changed the subject. And whenever Salma brought it up with Khalou, he told her it wasn't anything she needed to worry about. Since then, she's been having so much fun with her khalou, she's almost forgotten about the dinner anyway.

Over the past weeks, he has proven that he is,

indeed, the best khalou ever known to humanity. He's taken her on drives around town and let her play her favorite songs in his car. He got her a blue candy that turned her tongue a funny purple color, and he even gifted her his old tablet, so she can do all her drawings on its sleek screen with a funny-looking pen.

Today on the phone, Khalou and Salma plan a big trip to the amusement park when summer comes. He promises to ride the wooden roller coaster with her, and to buy her all the cotton candy she wants to eat.

"Salma," Mama calls. "Come help me with something!"

Salma says goodbye and finds Mama setting up a small ladder in the living room. She points to some spiderwebs by the ceiling. "Help me clean that up," Mama says.

"But I'm afraid of spiders!" Salma protests.

"Don't be." Mama smiles. "They are harmless and misunderstood."

Salma still doesn't want to get too close, so she holds the ladder for Mama to climb then hands her the broom and a cleaning cloth. When the spiderwebs are gone, Mama leans on the top of the ladder and takes a step down. Her foot misses the step. She gasps but holds on.

"Salma," Mama says meekly, "I feel dizzy."

Salma holds on to her mother's side, suddenly scared. "Are you okay, Mama?"

Mama carefully takes another step and stands on the floor again. Mama squeezes Salma's shoulder, but her hand feels weak. "I'll be fine. I think I just need to sit down."

"Maybe I should call Baba?" Salma's heart bounces in her chest.

"No need to worry him at work. Just help me to the couch."

When Mama sits, she leans back, closes her eyes, and holds on to her tummy. Salma notices her forehead is sweaty, so she rushes to the kitchen and runs some cold water on a tea towel. Mama dabs her face with it, but she doesn't seem any better.

Salma saw on TV that sometimes in an emergency, you need to call someone to help. But if she can't call her baba . . .

Suddenly, Salma knows exactly who to call.

Moments later, the doorbell rings, and Khalou Dawood walks in. Mama opens her eyes and blinks twice. "Dawood?" Her voice is weak. "What are you doing here?"

"I called him," Salma announces.

"Yes. I was buying groceries nearby, so I came right away," Khalou says in Arabic. This is the first time that Salma has heard him speak in his mother tongue. He steps into the kitchen and fills a water glass. "Salma said you weren't feeling well."

Mama shakes her head when Salma offers her the water.

"Drink it," Khalou Dawood says firmly. Salma pushes the glass closer to Mama.

Mama takes a few sips then sighs in relief. Khalou refills the glass and places it next to her. "Salma, will you help me make some food?" he asks, heading to the kitchen.

"Yes!" Salma is so happy Khalou is here. He knows what to do, and Mama already looks better.

"You don't need to worry yourself, Dawood," Mama says. Her voice is quiet and sweet. "I will be fine in a minute."

"Shush!" Khalou says, opening the fridge. "I would love to cook you breakfast today."

He pulls out some eggs, three tomatoes, and half an onion. He scratches his beard, thinking, then pulls out a bag of fresh mushrooms. He looks through the

spice rack then picks ground garlic, the seven spices mix, and some lemon pepper.

"Salma, where do you keep your mixing bowls?" he asks.

"Right here!" She grabs her favorite bowl; it's blue and has pretty dots on it.

"This will be the best omelet ever made," Khalou says, "but only with your help, Salma."

"I am a well-known Syrian chef," Salma jokes. "One day they will write books about my work."

They laugh, and Salma hears Mama laugh, too.

Soon, the sizzling of oil and the smell of fried eggs fill the house. Salma pokes her head around the corner to check on Mama.

"I feel so much better now, Salma," Mama says, patting the cushion next to her. "Thank you for taking care of me."

"What happened?" Salma asks as she sits beside her. "Why were you so dizzy?"

"Baba and I wanted to wait and tell you together, but I think you deserve to know right away," Mama says. She holds both of Salma's hands then places them on her belly.

"I am pregnant, Salma," Mama says. "You will be a big sister soon."

Salma's heart bounces, but this time, it's not

because she's afraid. Her eyes widen. "Mama, I will be the best older sister in the whole world!" she shouts.

"Mabrouk," Khalou Dawood says from the kitchen. "I wish you a healthy pregnancy, my dear sister." He leans in to give her a hug. Mama squeezes him in between her arms. Salma loves seeing them together like this.

"My new sibling and I will be so great together. Just like you and Khalou are the best siblings."

Mama giggles. "You are already the best older sister, Salma," she says.

"I will come up with a plan to be even better," Salma promises.

"Breakfast is ready," Khalou Dawood calls. "Come and get some yummy eggs!"

"Thank you," Mama whispers as Khalou slides the omelet onto small dishes. His face lights up.

While the three sit across from each other and eat the delicious omelet, Salma is filled with happiness. Life is wonderful when you have your family around you, and now their family is growing!

Chapter 3

A week later, Salma lies on a chair, her legs up against the back and her head hanging over the edge. She looks at the world upside down. Baba and Mama sit next to each other on the sofa, reading a book together.

Salma sighs. This is *so* boring. "Please can I watch TV?" she asks for the fifth time.

"Salma, we are trying to read an important book here," Baba says. "Reading in English is even more difficult than speaking it as a second language."

She sits upright, and rests her chin on her palms. Her parents

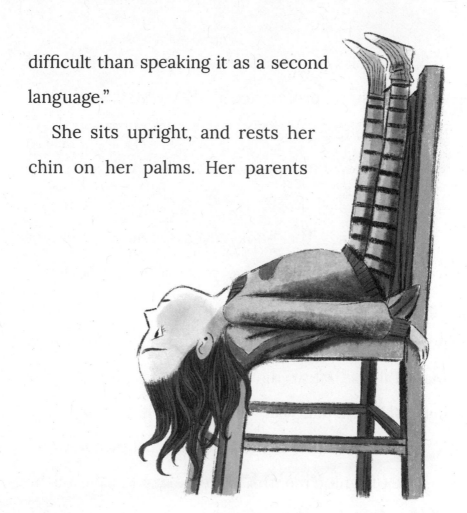

return to their book, licking the tips of their fingers and flipping pages quietly. Every now and then,

Baba stumbles on a word, leans into Mama's side and slowly tries to pronounce it. Then Mama explains the word to him.

"What are you reading that's so important, any- way?" Salma asks.

Mama raises the book cover. On it, a pregnant woman stands beside large white letters. She holds her belly lovingly, her hair brown and long. "It's a pregnancy book, my love," Mama says. "There are so many things that we didn't know about having a baby back when we had you."

Salma is confused. She thought all they had to do was wait for nine months, then she would have a baby sibling. Then, playtime: bike rides together, eating ice cream with big spoons, watching cartoons, and all sorts of fun adventures.

"You have to study for a baby?" Salma asks, pouting a little. "I thought it was easier than that."

"I wish," Mama says. "It's a lot of work to take care of a new baby. We want to make sure we have answers to any questions we might have."

Salma jumps off the chair. *There's a right and wrong way to raise a baby? That means there must be a right and wrong way to be a sibling!* Salma thinks.

"Slow down," Mama says, as Salma grabs the book. But Salma ignores her. She flips through it, trying to read its pages, and finds a mountain of words she doesn't recognize. She squints, hoping that she can focus enough to learn a word on the spot, but it doesn't help. Her shoulders drop, and she returns the book to Mama with a frown.

"How can I read this book?" Salma asks. "I also

have so many questions about how to be a good older sister!"

Baba laughs. He musses Salma's hair and pulls her in to sit between him and Mama. She cuddles in. "This is a grown-up book, Salma," Baba says. "It's about how the baby will grow inside Mama and how Mama will

feel—like why she was dizzy a few days ago. This book doesn't say anything about how to be a good sibling."

Salma grabs the book again and peers at the cover. She lifts it up next to Mama's face, comparing the cover model's brown hair to Mama's black, and her blue eyes to Mama's brown. "It's weird," she says. "This lady looks nothing like Mama. Are we sure this is the right book for us?"

"This is the book we could find, Salma." Baba takes the book back and flips the pages, looking for the one he was on before. "We need to be completely prepared for anything Mama and the new baby might need."

"I want to read about how to be a good sister," Salma insists. "I want to be there for my baby sibling and teach them everything they need to know about Syria and Canada."

"That's very important," Mama says. "Your future sibling won't have the same memories you have of Syria. You will be a great teacher and make sure they know everything about where we come from! You don't need a book for that."

But Salma isn't so sure. Being a big sister is a huge responsibility. There are a lot of things she'll need to teach her sibling.

This is the most important thing she'll ever do, and she needs to be completely prepared for it, like her parents.

She also knows that her family is unique: they have a long story to tell, one that includes crossing borders for a better life, and living in a place that's foreign to them, and making a home by mixing their Syrian history and their Canadian present. She really wishes she could read about how to be a good sister . . . but she doubts there is a book out there that is specific to her family.

Suddenly, Salma has the best idea ever.

"I will write my own book!" Salma announces.

Baba and Mama exchange a look. "You want to write your own book?" Baba asks.

"Yes. It will be a step-by-step guide on how to be a good older sibling."

"That's a great idea!" Mama says.

"I'll start right now!" Salma runs to her bedroom. She pulls a brand-new notebook off her shelf and gathers all her coloring pencils. She opens the first page and carefully writes out a title.

When she is done designing the cover with Syrian mosaic around its edges, jasmine flowers in its corners, and a big maple leaf right in the middle, she sighs happily.

Then, she realizes she has a problem. Salma has no idea how to write a book!

Chapter 4

All good guidebooks are based on research, examination, observation, and clear vision of the outcome. Salma reads the sentence again. *All good guidebooks are based on research, examination, obs—*

"What does examination mean here?" Salma whispers to Riya, who sits next to her in the school library at lunchtime. Riya reads the sentence, shrugs, and goes back to the novel she picked up for today.

"Also, what does it mean to have a clear vision of the outcome?" Salma scratches her head. "I don't understand anything here."

"*Shhhhhhh*," the teacher-librarian scolds from behind her desk. Salma dips her head into the book, then flips to the cover. The title says it teaches how to write books. She was reading the chapter about guidebooks, but none of it makes sense to her.

"I don't know how to write a good book, Riya." Salma covers her mouth with her palm so the librarian won't see. Riya just points at the signs telling students to be quiet.

"I just need to know how to write a good book so I can be the best older sister ever," Salma continues.

"You are not being the best quiet student in the

reading room right now, Salma," Riya whispers, also covering her mouth.

"*Shhhhhhhhhhhhhhhh!*" the teacher-librarian tilts her glasses and looks straight at Salma and Riya. The two lower their heads and pick up their books to hide their faces. Riya's face turns red, and Salma feels warmth in her cheeks.

She is stuck. She thought writing a book would help her learn how to be the best big sister. But writing a book is harder than she thought. There's so much to figure out before she actually puts pen to paper. She wishes writing wasn't this difficult. *How do authors write?* she wonders. *Do they get inspiration? Do they drink a lot of coffee and just type their thoughts on their fancy computers? Maybe they ask other authors for help, too.*

"Riya," Salma says, "do you know any authors? I need to ask them to—"

"Oh my god, Salma," Riya interrupts. "Be quiet!"

"Salma and Riya!" the teacher-librarian looks disappointed. "That's enough. You should return to your homeroom."

Riya frowns at Salma as she closes her novel and sets it on the librarian's desk. Salma follows her, eyes locked on the ground. Everyone stares at them as they leave.

Ms. Singh waves them into their classroom then returns to her lesson preparations. Riya is mad. She turns her back on Salma.

"I am sorry I got us in trouble, Riya," Salma apologizes. Riya looks back, rolls her eyes, and then sighs when she sees the look on Salma's face.

"It's okay," Riya says, smiling a little. "But you owe me a trip to the library to get that book back. This time, you have to stay quiet."

The two laugh and huddle closer, the way they always do. Salma looks out the window and sees some kids playing outside. There are the twins from Ms. Mariam's class, who hold hands even when they are running. On the slide, the Letofsky siblings play: the younger sister climbs the steps, while her two brothers wait for her at the end.

Maybe, Salma thinks, *I've been doing my research in the wrong place.*

"I think I need to interview everyone who has a sibling," Salma tells Riya. "One of the best ways to learn something new is to ask the experts."

She looks over at the fence, where the two new

sisters who joined the school recently sit alone. They eat their sandwiches next to each other, shoulder to shoulder, too shy to speak to anyone yet.

Salma turns around to find Riya already holding a large piece of paper, and two markers. "Let's come up with the questions together," Riya says. "We need to be prepared for our research."

Salma takes a marker, and for a moment she holds

Riya's hand. Sometimes, Salma feels that Riya is so close to her, she is like a sister. She is her best friend, her secret keeper, and the one who is and will always be next to her.

Questions for Nour! Salma writes at the top of the page.

"Who is Nour?" Riya asks.

"Oh, that's my nickname for my future sibling," Salma says. "Boys and girls—and anyone—can be named Nour. So, I decided to use it for now."

The two friends spread the piece of paper between them and start writing questions.

How do I make sure Nour knows they are loved? Salma writes. *How do I teach Nour to share their toys? How do I make sure Nour stays quiet in libraries?* Riya writes, and the two friends look at each other then giggle.

Chapter 5

Eid al-Adha is today, and everyone is ready for a celebration. Salma piles all the interview notes she made over the past weeks on her bed and heads to the kitchen to help Mama prepare their feast. Together, they stuff the soft and fluffy mamoul dough with dates and crushed nuts. Then, they put the desserts in the oven to bake.

Baba flips channels on the television until he finds one that plays the prayers from the Holy Mosque in Mecca. Salma joins him and sees his face light up with joy as praying men and women, dressed in white, walk around the mosque's center in circles united by their voices.

Salma loves Eid dinners. It's the time of the year when everyone in the family comes together for one large dinner, attended by all. She hasn't had one with her extended family since they left Syria, and this is also the first time Baba is here for this celebration in Canada. That's not all—it will be the first time Khalou is joining them for the feast. Salma is so excited!

When Khalou Dawood arrives, Salma hugs his waist, and he squeezes her close.

"Come right in," Salma says.

Khalou Dawood hesitates, then looks to his left. Her uncle brought a friend! He is also tall, with green eyes, blond hair, and a shy smile.

"Are those for me?" She points to the beautiful bouquet Khalou's friend is holding.

Khalou winks at her. "They're for your mama. Can you ask her to put her headscarf on?"

"Welcome to you and your friend," Mama says as she comes to the door, tightening her hijab.

Khalou Dawood puts his hand on his friend's waist as they step inside. "Everyone, this is my husband, Michael. Michael, this is my sister, Rima, and her family."

Mama freezes. Her hand pauses midair, inches away from a handshake.

"Dawood. What are you doing? We agreed not to bring this up."

Khalou takes a step back. He blinks fast, and his face turns red. He takes a deep breath. "Today is a day about family, sister. Michael is my family. He is my husband. We got married years ago."

"Congratulations, Khalou!" Salma jumps in. "I love weddings!" Weddings are the best! Salma loves them very much. She eats yummy desserts, and dances on the stage with all the other little girls. This is the first time she's heard about Michael, though. Isn't it weird that she never knew her khalou was married?

Salma feels her mother's hand on her shoulder. She looks up, and she can't tell what Mama is thinking. Is she confused? Maybe angry? Her expression reminds Salma of the time she broke Mama's favorite Damascene teacups. The ones they brought with them all the way from home.

Why is Mama disappointed in Khalou? Salma can't understand.

"Everyone is welcome," Baba says quickly. "Dinner will be ready soon."

"I brought these for you," Michael says, presenting the flowers to Mama. She looks at them for a moment, then puts them carelessly on the kitchen counter. She doesn't even say thank you.

"We will talk about this later," Mama insists, giving Khalou Dawood a look. Baba gestures for them to sit at the table.

Why would Mama be upset with Khalou Dawood for bringing his husband? Michael hasn't said anything yet, but he seems nice.

"Do you like Syrian food?" Salma asks Michael.

"Yes. Dawood cooks it for me all the time," he says. "He is an excellent chef."

"I love cooking, too!" Salma says, and Michael gives her a wink. "I even helped make tonight's dessert. Mama, did you and Khalou learn to cook when you were kids?"

But Mama just glares at her dish and breathes loudly. Salma had never seen her this mad before. It is weird to see her so angry. What if one day Salma makes a mistake, and Mama gets this mad at *her*? And what mistake did Khalou make, anyway?

"What did Khalou do wrong, Mama?"

"This is a grown-up thing, Salma," Mama says firmly.

"Is it because Khalou brought his husband?" Salma insists. Everyone's faces turn red.

Mama looks up from her food and stares straight at Khalou. "See what you did?"

Baba puts a soft hand on Mama's palm, but she pulls it away.

"Why didn't you tell us you were bringing Michael? And today of all days."

"I know you have a problem with who I love, Rima," Khalou says, calm at first, then louder as he speaks. "We come from a place where people are judged for who they love. But here in Canada everyone is equal no matter who they want to be married to."

The room is completely silent. No one is eating anymore. Salma is confused. Why would Mama be mad at Khalou for being in love with Michael? Mama loves Baba very much, and there is nothing wrong with that. Why is Khalou's love different?

"Maybe it was a mistake for me to come here today," Michael says slowly. He places his napkin on his half-full plate. "I am sorry. I don't mean to cause trouble for your lovely family."

Michael stands up and Khalou follows. "I will leave, too," he says.

"Oh, no!" Salma says. "Khalou, please stay. I wanted to show you the book I am working on. And you need to try our mamoul."

"Please stay." Baba stands, too. "I will make us some tea."

Salma turns to Mama, who is still sitting. "Mama, please tell Khalou to stay."

Mama is silent, and Salma's heart sinks.

"I love you, sister," Khalou says. "I hope one day you'll change your mind."

Khalou puts on his shoes. He leans on Michael a bit and shakes hands with Baba once more. Quietly, the two leave, and the door clicks closed behind them.

Chapter 6

Yesterday's dinner still weighs on Salma's mind, even on her way to school. It makes her sad to see Mama and Khalou fighting. What's worse is that she doesn't even completely understand what the problem is. She knows siblings sometimes get mad at each other. But this feels different.

One thing's for sure: Salma never wants to get this angry at her own sibling. But how can she prevent it if she doesn't even know what made Mama so mad? Nothing like this has come up in her guidebook research so far. What could Nour do that would make Salma that upset?

Salma knows she needs more help to finish her guidebook. She tucked it in her backpack this morning and pulls it out when she gets to her classroom. The room buzzes with excitement as the students pass

the book around. They marvel over Salma's drawings, and giggle at the funny quotes she collected from their schoolmates. The book is still filled with half-finished sketches and sticky notes with corrections and ideas.

"Is it okay to be mad at your sibling?" Salma asks the class, interrupting the chatter about the book.

"Maybe if my brother ate the last piece of chocolate

cake," Ayman says from the back of the room, and everyone laughs.

"I don't think brothers should be mad if one of them played with the other's toys, even if he broke it," one of the Letofsky siblings says.

"You destroyed our video game console," his brother says. "I'm allowed to be mad at you forever."

As the two siblings bicker about whose fault it is that they can't play video games anymore, Salma thinks about the fight between Mama and Khalou. She returns to her notes and research papers and flips through them, looking for clues. Maybe someone said something that can help her understand this situation.

"What's going on, Salma?" Ms. Singh asks. "You seem very distracted."

Salma tells Ms. Singh and all her friends about what happened at home last night. "I don't know why Mama would be so angry with my khalou," she says.

The students talk over each other, sharing their opinions. It's too much for Salma, and she sits back in her chair. Riya notices right away. She takes Salma's hand and squeezes it.

Ms. Singh knocks her knuckles on her desk, and the students quiet down. Salma notices the many ribbons and colorful papers her teacher uses in arts and crafts, and the lovely notebooks filled with ideas

and words Ms. Singh gathers for her lesson plans. Between the pens and pencils, Ms. Singh keeps a number of tiny little flags: a Canadian flag with its red and white strips, the British Columbia flag that Salma finds hard to draw, as well as a colorful rainbow flag.

"Sometimes, it is hard for us to imagine people living a life that's different from our own," Ms. Singh says.

"I just wish Mama wasn't so mad at Khalou," Salma says. "I love him very much, and I think Michael is wonderful, too."

Ms. Singh nods. She steps out from behind her desk and sits on Salma's table. "Sometimes, siblings fight," she says.

"I don't want to fight with my sibling at all," Salma insists. "I want to be the best older sister in the world.

I don't want to lose this love the way Mama lost her love for Khalou."

"The love your mama has for your khalou is like a beautiful sky," Ms. Singh says. "The clouds might come in every now and then and hide it, but the sky will always be there behind the clouds."

"How can I put this in the book?" Salma asks, still confused. "How can I make sure the love stays, even if people are angry?"

"Show us the book again, Salma," Ayman interrupts. "I want to see if you drew my black hair correctly."

"Who said she drew you in the book, Ayman?" Riya jokes.

"I am the most handsome boy in the whole world," he says proudly. "Of course she must have included me in there!"

Everyone laughs. Salma tightens her grip on her notes. She feels Riya's arm on her shoulder and leans into her friend's embrace. She is no closer to understanding what's going on between Mama and Khalou, and on top of this, she doesn't feel ready to write her guidebook anymore. Maybe the book was a bad idea. Maybe she won't be the best older sister in the world, after all.

Chapter 7

A few days later, Salma and Riya walk home together after school. Mama needs to go to the doctor for an ultrasound so they can take a picture of the baby. So, this afternoon, Salma is going to Riya's for a playdate. Salma feels the weight of her guidebook in her backpack, even though the papers are light.

"I don't know what to do anymore, Riya," Salma says as she sits on the fluffy carpet in Riya's room.

She spreads the papers between them like confetti. "I'm scared that if I don't finish the book, I won't be the best older sister. But I need to know how to be the best older sister in order to finish the book."

"Maybe you just need a break, Salma," Riya says. "How about we make a gift for Nour instead? Something that will show the baby how good of an older sister you are."

Salma is not sure. She needs to finish the book—it's the book she needs the most. Then, she decides that anything is better than staring endlessly at her notes. She nods in agreement, and for the next hour or so, they brainstorm gifts to make for the baby. Riya suggests they invent a new board game to play together, but Salma says it will be years before her sibling is old enough to play board games. Salma considers making them a skirt, but Riya reminds her that she doesn't know if the baby will want to wear skirts. They search online but don't find anything they like. Then Riya has an idea.

"All these baby photos have one thing in common," Riya says, pointing at their search results. "The babies are all wearing bibs. What if we sew a bib for your new sibling?"

"Of course!" Salma's eyes sparkle. Mama sews all the time and taught her how to sew by hand. A bib will look so cute when Nour is eating Salma's many cooking creations. Salma jumps up. "Do you have a sewing kit?"

"I have this one Maa got me," Riya says, "but I don't have any fabrics."

"Maybe we can find some around the house!" Salma races to the door.

The two girls sneak around the house. They hear Maa's voice coming from the living room, murmuring the lyrics of a song she likes. They look around the kitchen, but the tea towels are too thick. The bathroom rug is too wet. The curtains in the bedrooms are too high to remove. They're about to

give up, but then they go digging in Maa's closet.

"What about this?" Salma shows Riya a shawl she found all the way in the back. It's a beautiful red color, covered in tiny little golden birds. The fabric feels soft on the tips of her fingers. "It's so pretty."

"I've never seen this shawl before," Riya whispers back.

"Maa won't miss it then, right? It's perfect for a bib!"

Riya hesitates but follows Salma back to her bedroom. The two sit down and watch a video on how to make a bib. They have all they need: scissors, thread, and a small needle—and their fabric, of course. Salma holds the scissors open, about to cut into the shawl, when Riya holds out her hand.

"I don't know if this is a good idea, Salma," Riya warns. "Maybe we should ask Maa first."

Salma pauses. Maybe Riya's right. Maybe it's better to think twice before cutting someone else's shawl. Salma, however, can't help herself. If she can't finish her guidebook, she has to do *something* to show Nour that she's the best older sister in the world. And that something is making this bib with a beautiful fabric like this. Besides, Maa has lots of shawls. She probably won't even notice this one is missing.

"I think it's a great idea," Salma announces, and with that, she makes the first cut.

An hour later, the girls are surrounded by bits and pieces of the shawl, with no bib in sight. They tried everything and watched the video ten times, but the process was hard. The experiment has failed. Nothing Salma does seems to work anymore. She throws the

fabric scraps in the air in frustration, and they float down on her face softly.

"Riya, why did you go through my closet?" They hear Maa's voice from outside the bedroom door. "Did you take something from it?"

"What do we do?" Riya whispers in a frightened voice. She holds the ruined fabric. Salma is torn: maybe they should tell the truth, even if it will anger Maa. The truth, though, won't make things better. The shawl is destroyed, and there is no bib to replace it. Maybe they should lie and hide what they did. This way Maa won't be mad. Salma thinks of Mama's anger at Khalou Dawood. What if Maa gets that angry with Riya? And if Maa finds out, she'll tell Salma's mama. She could never forgive herself if she made Mama that mad.

What's the right choice here?

"I- I- I think you should lie," Salma whispers back. "Tell her we didn't take anything."

"Riya!" Maa's voice comes again. "What were you doing in my closet?"

Riya looks like she is about to cry. She stands up and squeezes her arms around her chest. "Nothing, we were just looking at your saris," she says, her voice shaking.

The girls listen. They hear an annoyed sigh. "Okay," Maa says, "but please ask first next time." Maa's steps fade away. They quickly gather the fabric pieces in a small plastic bag and hide it under Riya's bed. They don't talk to one another again until Mama comes to pick Salma up soon after.

On the way home, Salma wonders: *If Riya and I did the right thing not to anger Maa, why do I feel so bad?*

Chapter 8

After dinner, Salma heads straight to her room. With a red pen, she draws a large X in her guidebook, then another and another. Soon, the page is covered in Xs, and the words have disappeared under all the red lines.

"Stupid. Stupid. Stupid!" Salma scratches more red lines on the next pages.

It was a stupid idea to try to write this book. There is no way Salma can finish it. The job of an older sister is complicated, and full of surprises and responsibilities she never anticipated. She thought that being an older sister would be fun: walks on the seawall, swings in the playground, reading a book before bedtime. Turns out, it's much more than that. She has to learn how to make the right decisions, and how to teach her sibling the same. She has to learn how to guide her sibling, and how to be a role model. And worst of all, she still doesn't know when it is okay to be mad at your sibling, or how to fix things after a fight.

Salma rips out another page, crumples it into a ball, then throws it against the wall. It bounces and hits her on the head before falling to the floor. She groans, then lies down on the carpet. She covers her face with the papers.

The phone rings, and seconds later, Mama announces that it's Riya. Salma jumps up, sending the papers flying, then snatches the phone out of Mama's hand.

"Take it easy," Mama says as Salma closes her bedroom door.

"Maa noticed the shawl is missing, Salma," Riya whispers. "She was keeping it for a special occasion. I didn't know it was one of her favorites."

Salma holds the phone to her ear in silence. She feels its pressure on her face. She doesn't know what to do. Is it better to tell the truth, even when that means Maa will be mad, the way Mama is mad at Khalou? Or is it better to hide the truth and hope that Maa will forget about the shawl?

"Salma, are you there?" Riya whispers again.

"I'm sorry, Riya, I don't know the answer," Salma finally says.

The two friends remain on the phone for a moment. Neither of them says anything. Instead, Salma hears Riya pacing. She feels terrible. Her best friend, the closest person she has to a sister, has to choose between letting her mom down or lying to her. And it's all Salma's fault.

"I'm so sorry I got us into this mess," Salma says.

"Okay, Salma, I'll see you tomorrow." Riya sounds defeated. The line goes dead, and Salma is left alone in her room. She is frozen, the phone still to her ear. It takes all her energy to hold back tears.

"Salma, what's going on?" Mama cracks the door open. "You sounded really upset."

"Leave me alone, Mama." Salma pushes the door

closed and leans against it to keep it shut.

"Salma, let's talk about what's bothering you," Mama says from the other side.

"Everything is bothering me!" Salma shouts back. "I don't know how to finish the book, and I haven't collected any good lessons for being a good sister."

"I am sure I can help you with this," Mama says, "if you'd only open the door."

I also made Riya lie to her maa, Salma thinks, but she is afraid to say it out loud.

"I can't hear you, Salma," Mama says.

Salma pauses, then steps away from the door. Mama walks into the room.

"Whatever is going on," Mama says softly, "we can solve it together. I can teach you how to be a good older sister."

Salma feels the heat of anger gathering in her chest like lava, then it explodes like a volcano. "No. You can't help me!" Salma's back and shoulders tense up. "You are so confusing, Mama."

"What?"

"Sometimes you love Khalou Dawood," Salma continues, "and sometimes you are mad at him, and I don't understand how you can be a good older sister if you can't even be friends with your own brother. What did Khalou do that was so bad, anyway? Why can't he love Michael?"

Mama takes a step back. "This is a grown-up issue," she says.

"I will grow up one day!" Salma shouts, then jumps in her bed, turning her back on her mother. "And I will be the worst older sister in the world. Just like you."

Salma expects Mama to say something. Instead, she hears the bedroom door close. When she looks back, she is alone in her room. Salma feels tears rolling down her face. She finally did it. She made Mama mad at her, the way she is mad at Khalou.

Today is the worst day of Salma's whole life.

Chapter 9

It's nighttime, and Mama hasn't spoken to Salma since their argument earlier. When Baba walks in after work, Salma's parents whisper in the living room for a bit. When Mama comes into her bedroom, Salma is sure she is in trouble. She might even be grounded. Instead, Mama hands her the phone.

"Your khalou is on the line," Mama says. Salma approaches her, wanting to talk, but Mama pushes the phone forward. "Go talk to him in the living room, please," she says firmly.

Salma holds the phone for a moment and looks up at Mama. Then, she puts the phone to her ear and whispers a hello.

"Hey, Salma." She hears Khalou's voice. "What's going on? Are you okay?"

Salma can't help herself: she starts crying right away and tells her uncle everything. The guidebook she hoped to write, the conversation she shared at school, and what happened at Riya's. Finally, in an embarrassed voice, she tells him about her fight with Mama.

"That's a lot of heavy things for one girl to think about." Khalou Dawood's voice makes her feel calmer. "Even if she's the tallest girl in her class."

"I am just so confused," Salma says. "I don't know how to be a good older sister. I don't know why Mama is not a good older sister to you either."

Khalou is silent for a moment. "Salma, I need you to know some things about your mama. When we were growing up, she was the best sister."

Khalou Dawood tells Salma of the many things he loves about her mother: the games they played together growing up, the times she helped him with his homework or answered the silly questions he was too embarrassed to ask anyone else. The way she held his hand in the Damascus airport right up until they

said their goodbyes, and the way she hugged him so hard when he finally saw her again.

"Your mother tried to understand when I first told her about Michael," Khalou says, his voice quiet. "We have had many conversations about it. Before you were born, when you were a baby, and again now that you are old enough to hear us."

"Why wouldn't Mama just be happy for you and Michael, Khalou?" Salma asks.

"It's hard for her, because when I tell her my love is right, everyone else back in Syria tells her that my love is wrong," Khalou explains. "She is as confused as you are, Salma. Mama has made some mistakes in dealing with her confusion, the same way you made a mistake at Riya's."

Salma sits quietly in the living room, listening to her

khalou. Her head spins as she thinks about cutting up Maa's shawl. She should have been honest, and asked Riya to be honest, too. And she should have asked Maa about the shawl before taking it. She can definitely understand now how confusion and fear can lead to mistakes.

"Back in Syria, even with the whole world telling your mama that I am wrong, that my love for Michael is wrong, she still loved me," Khalou continues. "She disagreed with me—she still disagrees with me—but she still loves me." Khalou adds, "I was also confused, and I made the mistake of bringing Michael to meet you without talking to my sister first."

"I don't like how the two of you are not happy with one another," Salma admits. "How can Mama be a good older sister if you two are not talking to each other?"

Khalou explains that sometimes, it takes time for us to understand our mistakes. Sometimes, we have to be brave enough to do the right thing. "But, being a good person doesn't mean not making mistakes at all, it means knowing when you make a mistake, and trying to fix it. I hope your mama will get there soon." He adds, "Maybe I should be a good younger sibling and wait patiently until she is ready."

"It seems that we have all made a lot of mistakes lately," Salma says.

"Yes," he agrees, "but we are solving this now, by talking to each other from a place of love. Promise me to talk to your mother about your feelings, Salma, and to fix things with Riya."

Salma nods and agrees. She feels a new wave of energy filling her heart. She thanks Khalou for listening and promises to talk to him soon.

She finds Mama and Baba in her bedroom, sorting through what's left of her guidebook. Mama has uncrumpled the pages Salma scrunched up and smoothed them out in front of her. Baba has collected the rest of the pages in a neat pile. He hands her the pile, ruffles her hair, then steps outside, closing the door behind him. For a few moments, Salma doesn't know what to do or say. Finally, she sits down next to Mama.

"Mama, I am so sorry I spoke to you in a bad way," Salma says.

"Salma, I am sorry I didn't realize how my actions were affecting you." Mama opens her arms for Salma. "Maybe we solve this with a hug?"

Salma rushes into her mother's embrace. She closes her eyes, and smiles when she smells Mama's scent:

a mix of her jasmine perfume, her lilac shampoo, and cardamom. "I wish Khalou Dawood was here, too," Salma whispers. "He told me how much he loves your warm hugs."

"Salma, I love your uncle so much." Mama looks Salma in the eyes. "I want to give him a hug every time I see him. It has been difficult being his older sister because I feel torn between loving him and all the values we grew up with."

"Isn't there some place in the middle between these two things?" Salma asks. "You always tell me that the best solutions are the ones where everyone is happy."

Mama smiles. She pulls Salma in for a second hug. When Salma looks up, she sees tears in her mother's eyes. She worries, but then notices Mama's soft smile. "When did you grow up to be such a smart girl, Salma?" Mama teases. "Now you're teaching me lessons about being a good sister."

Salma feels proud and her mother's words fill her with joy. She never knew she had the power to change her mother's mind, but maybe she does. Not through lying and hiding, but through honesty and love.

Mama collects more of Salma's pages and looks at them intently. She examines the big red Xs and the hard lines Salma drew. She looks as if she is thinking deeply, then her face brightens up. "It has been so serious around here. Maybe we can have a little get-together next weekend. Us three, and Riya and her maa, and Khalou Dawood, too," Mama says. "Call your uncle and ask if he can join us!"

"Both him and Michael?" Salma stands up. Mama hesitates. She frowns and bites her lower lip. She takes a deep breath, then nods a yes.

"Before the party, we have to go to the market together," Salma insists. "I need to buy a new shawl for Riya's mother." Mama raises her eyebrows as Salma explains what happened that afternoon.

Khalou was right: it's not about never making mistakes; it's about being brave enough to fix them. This evening, Salma is ready to fix her mistakes.

Chapter 10

Salma is hosting a party, and her home is ready for all her guests to arrive. Salma wears a dress covered in little penguins that her mama made her for this occasion, and her hair is tied up in a long, bouncy ponytail. Mama wears a hijab made from the same fabric, and the penguins look like they are dancing whenever she laughs. Baba pulls a few kibbeh out of the frying pan every now and then, before dropping more of the round balls of meat and bulgur in the hot oil.

Riya arrives first with her maa. Salma is ready with a gift. A shawl, as beautiful as the old shawl the girls destroyed, wrapped in green paper.

"I am so sorry for what I did at your home, Maa," Salma says. "I am sorry I got Riya to lie, too."

Maa accepts the gift gracefully, then leans down to the two girls. "Even when you do something wrong, we mothers will always love you. No matter what happens, you can always talk to us."

Salma and Riya nod. Salma is glad she admitted her fault and fixed her mistake. She knows it doesn't mean the mistake never happened. It just means that it's now been solved, with love.

Maa tells them to go and play together. "No scissors

this time around," she warns, but she is smiling.

Salma keeps one eye on the door, impatient for the last two guests to get there. A few minutes later, a large box fills the doorway. Salma recognizes the long legs behind it.

"Khalou Dawood!" she yells.

"Oh, brother, you shouldn't have," Mama says.

"It's no bother at all," he says in Arabic. He slowly

places the box on the floor in the hallway, pauses to catch his breath, then opens his arms to Salma, who rushes in for a big hug.

Salma is disappointed. *Where is Michael? Maybe he's not coming?* She needs to be patient, Salma remembers. She needs to wait until her mama is ready to embrace Khalou and his husband. It might be hard for Khalou, and it will be a lot of work for Mama, too, but Salma knows now how much they love each other. The waiting and the effort will be worth it.

"I am still the tallest girl in my class," Salma says, trying to lighten up her thoughts. "Maybe I will play basketball next year!"

"I would love to see that." Khalou Dawood musses Salma's hair.

"Hey! Watch my ponytail. Mama spent a long time on my hair today!" Khalou pinches her cheek and she giggles.

"I got you a gift," he says. "This is a writing desk so you can write all the books you want to, Salma. It needs to be assembled, but Michael and I will help you with it."

Khalou Dawood looks behind him. "Michael, are you coming in?"

Michael appears in the doorway. He came after all! He waves shyly and says a quick hello but stays by the door. Salma wants to drag him in as soon as possible: she doesn't like to see how shy he looks. *Patience*, she reminds herself. *Maybe Mama has something to say.*

"Hello, Michael," Mama says, after a moment of hesitation. She looks as shy as Michael. "Please come in."

"Thank you so much," Salma says, examining the big box. "I can't wait to work at my new desk! I feel like a real author already."

Mama shows Khalou the way into Salma's room. Michael seems a bit lost. Salma holds out her hand and asks him if he wants to be introduced. He nods a polite yes. She pulls him over to Riya and Maa. They stop talking and look at the tall man Salma just brought in.

"Everyone, this is Michael," she says. "He is my khalou's husband."

Riya's maa smiles politely while Riya shakes Michael's hand. Baba comes in from the kitchen and gives Michael a hug, patting him twice on the shoulder.

"Welcome to the family," Baba says, loud enough for everyone to hear.

"Thank you," Michael says. He looks down at Salma. "And thank you for introducing me, Salma. You're very sweet."

"Salma is the best," Khalou says from the hallway. Salma's heart glows when she sees his hand intertwined with her mama's. "She will grow up to be the best older sister in the world, I hear. Show us your guidebook, Salma!"

Salma runs back to her room. She opens her drawer and pulls the book out. She redid the first couple of pages that she tore apart, glued some of them together, and redrew her designs on others. She added some new lessons, too. She likes the one she learned from her khalou best. She reads it to herself: *Even when we disagree, we still have love for one another.*

She flips the pages. It's not finished yet, but that's okay. She will fill the empty pages with all the lessons she will learn over the years. She might even pass the book down to her own sibling one day. Who knows!

Salma hugs the book close to her chest, then runs out to show it to all the people she loves.

How to write a book like Salma!

Salma loved writing her first book so much, she wants to write a hundred more. Her sibling guidebook was non-fiction, but now Salma wants to use her imagination to invent new stories. What will she write next? Maybe she will write a story about a princess who can save her kingdom all by herself. Maybe she will write a story about a star that fell to Earth and wants to find its way back to the sky. Maybe she will write a story that no one's ever thought of before. And you can write your own story, too!

Here are some questions to get you started:

1. What is the name of your main character?

2. Your main character can be a person, an animal, or an imaginary creature. It doesn't matter, as long as they really, really want something and are adventurous.

3. Where will this story take place?

4. Tell your reader more about the surroundings of your main character. It could be something as familiar as your classroom, or something as imaginative as a spaceship. It's all up to you.

5. What is your main character's goal?

6. Your main character needs to have a good reason why they do what they do. What do they want? Why does it matter so much to them?

7. What is your main character's biggest challenge?

8. Every hero needs a challenge to rise above. What makes it hard for your character to reach their goal? Who or what stands in their way? How will they overcome these challenges?

9. How will your story end?

10. A good ending makes the book even better! What will happen to your main character? Will they reach their goal? We can't wait to find out.

To get to know your character more, you might want to try to walk in their shoes. For this part, pretend you are your main character, and fill in the blanks with your own ideas right here:

I am a story character and my name is _____.
I am_____ years old. I come from a place called
_____, and it's my favorite place in the world because _____.
My favorite _____is _____.

My best friend's name is _____. This friend knows me well because we _____ together all the time. My favorite thing about my friend is _____.
However, sometimes it bothers me that my best friend

_____.

On my big adventure, I want to _____.
This will help me find _____. It will also help my family and friends know that I am _____

_____.

Now that you know your character well, it's time to write your book. Here are the supplies you need:

- A notebook you love.

- Pens, pencils, and an eraser.

- Coloring pencils, pens, or markers in case you want to do your own illustrations.

- A collection of books that inspired you, including all of Salma's adventures.

Keep reading for a sneak peek of

Joins the Team

Coming in 2024!

978-1-77321-828-1 HC
978-1-77321-829-8 PB

Chapter 1

Salma has a big question to ask, but she doesn't know where to start. She hovers in her bedroom doorway, watching Mama breastfeed her new baby sister, Nora, in the living room.

"Hi, Salma. Do you need anything?" Mama asks while the baby coos.

"Nope. Nothing," Salma says, losing her nerve.

"Well, it feels like there is something," Mama says

playfully. She pats the couch beside her. "Come sit with us."

Salma pauses, then crosses over to sit by Mama's side. She bounces her legs on the couch, still not sure how to bring this up with her mother. Mama tightens the shawl around Nora, then looks Salma in the eye.

"Salma," Mama says, "what do you want?"

It's *now or never*, Salma thinks. "Mama, you know how much I love Yusra Mardini right?"

Mama nods. "Of course." Over the past few months, Mama helped Salma redecorate her room: there are pictures of Mardini standing by the Olympic torch, a poster of her bundled up in a towel after winning a qualifying swimming race, and a little replica of an Olympic gold medal hanging on the wall.

"Well, today I shared a video of her with my class."

Salma pictures it: The swimmer standing proudly at the edge of the pool. She doesn't look nervous. Like Salma, she has light tanned skin with some dimples and birthmarks. A wisp of hair—chestnut brown, just like Salma's—escapes her swim cap. Her eyes are the color of honey, Salma knows, even though Yusra is wearing goggles.

"All my friends loved Yusra," Salma insists.

She remembers her friend Riya turning to her in excitement when the video finished. "Yusra is so cool. She went through so much, but now she's thriving!"

"It's very common for immigrants and refugees to be successful when given the chance," Ms. Singh said.

"Yusra is my new favorite Olympian," Ayman added. "I don't know any other Olympians, but she is my favorite for sure."

Even though she'd seen the video many times, Salma's eyes had been glued to the big screen, watching her hero doing the butterfly—breaking the surface of the water, and splashing it gently everywhere.

"I wish I could swim like Yusra," Salma told her classmates.

And that's when Ms. Singh had shared the most amazing thing ever. The thing Salma needs to ask Mama about now.

"Maybe you can be like Yusra!" Ms. Singh had said. "There's a swimming club in the school!"

Salma doesn't know how to swim and no one in her family has ever been to a swimming pool. But Ms. Singh had explained that she could learn to swim in the club. If she worked hard, she could even try out for the school swim team. And if she made it onto the team, she'd get to race against other schools!

All she needs is her parents' permission.

Salma leans into Mama's side and lets images of her possible future fill her head. She, too, could jump elegantly into the swimming pool. She could push the water with her arms and legs until she floats on its surface like a butterfly. She could win all the Olympic medals in the world and carry them around her neck proudly.

"That's nice, Salma." Mama's voice breaks into her thoughts. "It's always wonderful to share your interests with friends. But was there something else you wanted to ask me?"

Salma takes a deep breath. She is scared to ask her

question. What if Mama says no? But there's only one way to find out.

"Mama, I want to join the school swim club," she says in a rush. She shares what Ms. Singh told her. Mama leans back and rocks the baby softly. Then she gets up and puts Nora in her crib.

"Mama? Why aren't you answering?" Salma asks. "Are you afraid I will drown?"

"Oh. Don't say that. Of course not," Mama says, busying herself with the dishes. "You are a strong girl, and I am sure the school has many lifeguards."

"Then what is it, Mama?" Salma pulls at Mama's robe. Mama sighs. She turns off the tap and bends down to Salma's eye level.

"Honestly, Salma, the problem is that our religion and traditions say that girls cannot wear revealing outfits in public," Mama says. "That includes the swimsuit you will have to wear if you join this sport."

Wait, what? Salma's never thought about that before. She wears long sleeves more often than most of the other girls at school, and she has a section of her closet for the clothes she can wear to the mosque. But she's never really thought about why ... or that wearing a swimsuit would be a problem. "I don't understand. Yusra wears a swimsuit all the time."

"There are many different cultures, religions, and traditions in Syria. We come from a more traditional background than Yusra." Mama reminds Salma of the other Syrian women they meet when they go to the mosque. They wear long sleeves, and long skirts, too. And they all wear the hijab around their heads like

Mama. "For Syrians like our family and the people who go to our mosque, wearing a swimsuit could be seen as disrespectful."

Salma doesn't want to be disrespectful. She loves going to the mosque—it's the only time she meets other Syrian girls, as none of them go to her school. But she wants to be like Yusra Mardini, who is also a Syrian girl, even if she is from a different background. It's not like Salma would wear her swimsuit to the mosque!

"Please just think about it, Mama." Salma channels Yusra's determination. "I really want to be part of this swimming team. It means the whole world to me, Mama."

Mama's face softens. She pulls Salma in for a hug and kisses her on the forehead. "I will think about it,

Salma," Mama says. "I will discuss it with Baba and let you know what we decide."

Salma nods. She will do whatever her parents think is best, but she hopes they will make the right decision and let her swim.

About the Author

DANNY RAMADAN made Canada his home in 2014 after leaving his homeland of Syria and becoming a refugee in Lebanon. Since then, Danny has written multiple books for both kids and grown-ups. People seem to think Danny knows how to write well. To his surprise, they keep asking him for more books.

In Vancouver, the place Danny calls home, he met Matthew, the love of his life, and married him. The two adopted the bestest dog in the world, Freddie, who is named after a singer from the '80s you are too young to know and who naps exclusively in Danny's lap every afternoon. When Danny is not writing, he is playing video games.

About the Illustrator

Just like Salma, ANNA BRON moved to Canada with her family when she was very young. She remembers helping her parents with English and making friends in school with kids from all over the world. She always loved to draw from her imagination and when she grew up, she became an illustrator and animator. She gets to work on lots of fun projects, from drawing kids' books to designing unique characters and working on short animated films. Her favorite things to draw are horses, birds, and mountains. When she's not drawing, she loves getting outside to hike and ski.